DOROTHY & MIKEY

KEIKO KASZA

G. P. PUTNAM'S SONS · NEW YORK

Library of Congress Cataloging-in-Publication Data
Kasza, Keiko. Dorothy and Mikey / Keiko Kasza.   p.   cm.
Summary: Three stories featuring Mikey and Dorothy, two friends who play
and compete with one another. [1. Friendship—Fiction. 2. Play—Fiction.
3. Competition (Psychology)—Fiction.] I. Title. PZ7.K15645Ds 2000 [E]—dc21
98-18318 CIP AC ISBN 0-399-23356-3 10 9 8 7 6 5 4 3 2 1 First Impression

*For **Refna Wilkin**,*
my editor and friend

THE KNIGHT AND THE PRINCESS

Dorothy and Mikey are best friends. . . . well, most of the time.

One day, they read a book called *The Knight and the Princess*.

"Let's play," said Mikey. "I'll be the knight, and you be the princess."

"Great!" said Dorothy.

"I'll save you from the bad guys, okay?" said Mikey.

"No way!" shouted Dorothy. "What's wrong with the princess saving the knight?"

They argued and argued until finally Mikey said, "I'm not playing with you anymore."

"Good,"said Dorothy. And she went home.

Mikey was determined
to have fun all by himself.
He drew pictures. Lots of
pictures. "Who needs
Dorothy?" he said.

He read his bug book.
Fourteen times. "I'm
not bored," he said.
"Who needs her?"

Then he got an idea. "I'll show that Dorothy," Mikey

thought. "I can play *Knight and Princess* all by myself."

Knight Mikey announced to all the people in the kingdom, "I shall fight the bad guys, and save our princess."

He galloped through the battlefield . . .

. . . he fought bravely with
the bad guys . . .

. . . and he saved the princess,
which was really a log.

But the Princess Log didn't say a word.

Mikey looked at the log and said, "You should say,

'Thank goodness you are here, you handsome knight!'"

He dropped the log and sighed. "That's what Dorothy

would say."

"No, I wouldn't," yelled a voice from behind the

bush. "I would say, 'What took you so long?'"

It was Dorothy, dressed like a princess.

"Dorothy," shouted Mikey, "am I glad to see you!"

"No, Mikey," said Dorothy, "*I'm* glad to see *you*.

Playing alone was so boring."

The rest of the day, they took turns saving each other from the bad guys. Then Knight Mikey and Princess Dorothy galloped back to the kingdom together and played happily ever after . . . well, most of the time.

BRAGGING

One day Mikey started bragging.

"I can jump higher than you."

"Oh, yeah?" said Dorothy.

"I can run faster than you."

"Oh, yeah?" said Dorothy.

"I can stand on one foot longer than you."

"Oh, yeah?" said Dorothy. "Then show me."

First they tried to jump up to a branch. Mikey
was able to grab on to it, but Dorothy couldn't.

"Na na na naaana," Mikey teased. "You see,
I can jump higher than you."

Next they raced to the top of a hill. Mikey got there ahead of Dorothy.

"Na na na naaana," Mikey teased again.

"Told you, I'm faster than you."

Then Mikey and Dorothy each stood on one foot like a scarecrow. After a few minutes, Dorothy lost her balance and fell over. Mikey won again.

"Na na na naaana. The kid never loses. He does it again!" Mikey went on and on.

Dorothy was mad, but then she thought of something.

"Hey Mikey, let's play that scarecrow game again,"

said Dorothy. "But this time with our eyes closed."

"Sure, if you want to lose again," sneered Mikey.

"We'll see who gets the last laugh," Dorothy answered.

"Ready, steady, go!"

As soon as Mikey closed his eyes, Dorothy
tiptoed home.

All through the hot afternoon, Mikey stood
sweating in the field, bragging away all the while.
"I'm faster than you, Dorothy, and I can jump
higher, too. . . . "

"Yes, all that's true," thought Dorothy, as she sat

down to a cool lemonade. "But who's smarter, kid?"

THE POEM

One day, Dorothy found Mikey rolling in the mud.

"That looks like fun, Mikey. Can I join you?" she asked.

"No," replied Mikey, "I must do this alone."

Dorothy was upset. "Huh! You're not very friendly today."

The next day, Dorothy found Mikey swimming
with a frog.

"That looks like fun, Mikey. Can I join you?"
she asked.

"No," replied Mikey, "I must do this alone."

Dorothy was mad. "Huh! You're not very
polite today."

The next day, Dorothy found Mikey sitting in a box.

"That doesn't look like fun, Mikey. You need company?" asked Dorothy.

"No," replied Mikey, "I must do this alone."

Now Dorothy was furious. "You've been so mean to me. Why?!"

"I'll tell you tomorrow," said Mikey.

"Gee, I can hardly wait," Dorothy sputtered.

The next day, Dorothy stomped into Mikey's house
and slammed the door.

"All right, Mikey," she yelled, "what's going on?"

Mikey answered, "I just had to be alone,
Dorothy. You see, I was writing a poem."

She snatched the piece of paper
and began to read:

Dorothy

I like Dorothy.
She's really, really fun,
like rolling in the mud,
or swimming with a frog.

Without Dorothy,
I'd be really, really sad,
like sitting all alone
in a dark, quiet box.

She's sometimes a pest
But it doesn't bother me
'Cause I like Dorothy,
as anyone can see.

By Mikey

"Oh, Mikey!" Dorothy screamed and gave him a big hug. "The poem is wonderful."

"Thanks," said Mikey proudly. They pinned the poem on the wall and admired it together.

"Now," said Mikey, "let's go play in the mud!"

"Sure," said Dorothy, "but you go on ahead, and I'll join you in a minute."

As soon as Mikey left, Dorothy grabbed a pen and made a little change in the poem.

Dorothy

I like Dorothy.
She's really, really fun,
like rolling in the mud,
or swimming with a frog.
Without Dorothy,
I'd be really, really sad,
like sitting all alone
in a dark, quiet box.
~~She's sometimes a pest.~~ She's always the best.
But it doesn't bother me
'Cause I like Dorothy,
as anyone can see.

By Mikey

"Now it's perfect," Dorothy murmured.

Then she dashed out to play with Mikey.